THE SECRET OF THE OHKS

Published in Canada by Engen Books, St. John's, NL.

ISBN-13: 978-1-77478-015-2

Distributed by:
Engen Books
www.engenbooks.com
submissions@engenbooks.com

First mass market paperback printing: February 2021

Cover Design: Ellen Curtis

Slipstreamers Committee:
Amanda Labonté
Ali House
AJ Ryan
Ellen Curtis
Erin Vance
Lauralana Dunne
Matthew LeDrew

THE SECRET OF THE OHKS

AJ RYAN & JD RYOT

ENGEN BOOKS

CHAPTER ONE

Shouts erupted close behind as Cassidy beat a path through the tall grass. She huffed and puffed, pushing her legs to the limit, shoving through the huge blades of green. The local strong arms were hot on her heels. She could hear several pairs of feet crashing through the grasses as well.

She finally broke out of the line of green, making for the blue cobblestone road. The road led downward, between the halves of a rocky hill. It had been cut open to build the road through it instead of going around. She glanced over her shoulder, seeing the guards with their red capes flapping behind them as they gained on her. She just had a little further to go. She pushed what little reserve she had left to bolster her on down the road.

At last, the bridge came into sight. She thumped along the boards, feeling the structure stretch a little, but the tight ropes held strong. She glanced back again and saw her pursuers were gathering at the edge of the bridge, but not following. She frowned, scrunching up her bright eyes as she brought her attention back ahead of her. That's when she stumbled to a halt.

Waiting on the other side was a similar group, except they were clad in blue. Two opposing peoples. Neither likely to let her through in peace. She looked behind her at the Red capes. They were pointing at her, shouting in their long syllables.

"Sorry?" she held up her hands.

Shouts began on the other side. She whirled around. These guys were quicker at making decisions. They were already marching onto the bridge. The shouts gained a new pitch behind her. She could already guess why, but she looked anyway.

Just as she expected, they were also beginning a march onto the bridge. They increased their strides.

The Blues did too.

The Reds compensated, breaking into sprints.

"Only one way out," she thought aloud, waiting until her blood hammered through her veins at the same fast tempo. She ducked under a rope, drew in a quick breath and sprung off the bridge, swan diving towards the waters below.

"Professor Cane?"

"Hm?"

"The water table tablets, right?"

"Huh?" Cassidy looked out into the lecture theatre where only half the seats were filled. The department head had noted a fall in the numbers for her classes. She had received an email from him before class. She was going to be audited. She blinked hard, bringing herself back into the present.

"Oh. Yes. Correct. That was the artifact we were hunting for. And, uh, who was the pivotal researcher that led us to the most likely area?"

A half-dozen hands raised. She pointed to the closest student. However, the voice faded out, her eyes no longer interested in what was beyond the tip of her own nose. The boredom was like a massive blanket, muffling every-day life.

Then she was in her office, but she didn't remember going there; not one part of the journey.

Autopilot.

Mundane life just ran on its own for Cassidy Cane nowadays. She had passed on the last expedition that had come her way. She had something way more exciting on the horizon. Or she thought she had. Gamgee had hinted at another portal about to clear for her, but that had been over a month ago.

She sat back in her chair, making it squeak as she leaned into the cushions, thinking. All she got was irritation and maddening expectation. Did you bring a skydiver up into the air and forbid them to jump? She actually didn't know the real answer to that, but her point still stood. Her eyes caught sight of the papers on the end of her desk. Essays that she had yet to read. Cassidy found her attention ran away whenever she tried to comb through them.

She clasped her hands together, her fingers feeling along the line of a scar on her palm as she attempted to concentrate, even a little. On the shelves of her tight of-fice were trinkets from her earthly adventures, A chunk of amber from the British Isles, a fossil from Mexico, and a polished disk from a dig site in Africa. However, there was one that did not belong to the same category. It had no earthly origin. It looked to be a piece of glass with dyes caught in it. Though the outside was solid, the inside appeared viscous. Blue and red swirled like ink in dense water, only briefly mixing and then pushing apart again.

She groaned upon glancing over her collection. "This is impossible." She pushed herself onto her feet, hauled on her worn leather jacket and made for the door.

It opened before she could reach it. Cassidy took a quick step back as Margo stepped in. Seeing her big sister standing before her, Margo quickly shut the door behind her. "Going out?" she asked.

"Margo, what are you doing here?" Cassidy asked instead of answering. Her mind ran through a bunch of possible scenarios in the meantime.

Her sister sighed, crossing her arms. "I told Mom you were checked out."

"Huh?"

"Yep," she agreed with herself, walking over to the nearest shelf. Cassidy began to feel the judgement rolling off her middle sister. It really didn't rub well with her.

"You totally forgot I was coming for a visit." She outlined, "You probably have other plans, too." She picked up an artifact and turned it over in her hand. It was a little stone statue Cassidy had brought back from South America.

"As a matter of fact," Cassidy reclaimed the artifact from her grasp and put it back where it belonged.

"Running off on another big trip?" Margo continued to lead on, her hint of sarcasm hitting Cassidy square in the face.

"Well it *is* part of my job," she shot back, forceful enough to say that Margo should have put those facts together by now.

"Doing your job is one thing, Cass, but this pace is something else altogether."

"Geez, Margo, you've really been working on the theatrics." Cassidy almost groaned with flat wit.

Margo shot her a glare only a sister could appreciate.

"What are you trying to say?" Cassidy rested her hands on her hips.

"You've always been fast. Remember how you used to drag me when I was a toddler? You could never just walk anywhere." She shook her head, "but lately you've been ratcheting up even more than usual."

"Okay. So, I live fast." Cassidy shrugged, then crossed her arms over her chest, still waiting for a logical problem to be presented to her.

"More than that, Cassidy. Ever since Dad got sick, you've gone off to places that are more remote, and much more dangerous. Now after Dad's relapse, it's like you are constantly taking these trips to unknown places without hardly a break."

"I think I can thank you for your concern, at least it seems like concern, but there's nothing wrong with any of my work." Cassidy took hold of her shoulder to direct her out of the way of her door.

Margo steadied herself in place instead of being ushered out. "What are you running from?"

"What?" Cassidy edged to a stop, hesitating, wondering whether she should look at her sister directly or not.

"Or maybe you think you're running to something?" Margo thought again. Then she shook her head, meeting Cassidy's gaze.

"Rica says you've always been racing ahead of yourself, but that's not true. You might have been determined, but lately you're pulling away. It's like you're becoming someone else. You're obsessed with whatever it is you say you're chasing, or running away from," Margo explained simply. Somehow, her words dug into Cassidy.

"I have to keep on top of things in my job." Cassidy's statement came out in a defensive tone, giving Margo license to drive forth in her own righteousness.

"You need to slow it down, Cass. No one can race indefinitely."

"Look, I'm sorry I got our schedules mixed up, but I have somewhere I have to be." Cassidy reached around her, taking her time so that Margo could sidestep out of her way at last. "I can email you a list of the good restaurants in town."

"Wow, Cass." Margo leaned her weight to one side, arms crossing again.

Cassidy waved her toward the door and straight into a young man.

"Oh, sorry." He stepped back, fiddling with the papers he held in his hands.

"It's okay." Margo eased up, speaking gentler toward him than she had to her eldest sister.

"Professor Cane," he stepped up to Cassidy as she was closing the door to her office.

"Yeah?" She looked him over. He didn't look familiar to her.

"I was wondering if we could talk."

"Sorry. I have another engagement. Next time you can email me to schedule office time," she said, then zipped up her coat.

"But - but we did schedule a time," he stammered.

She paused. Then she hesitated on going back to her office. The mundane blanket over her shoulders felt too suffocating. She had a mission to get. Something to blow this stuffy slow pace of life right off her.

"Sorry. We'll have to re-schedule." She worked to keep Margo from catching her gaze as she quickened her pace down the hall.

"Sorry if I took up your time." Cassidy could hear her sister speaking to him as she pulled open the door to the stairs. It didn't matter.

CHAPTER TWO

She got herself to the lab of Dr. Herbert Gamgee straight away. She'd sat with the uncomfortable and prosaic pace long enough.

"Gamgee," Cassidy called as she entered his warehouse lab. She looked down from the walkway above, but found that he was not in the fishbowl space below. Brushing a loose piece of her red hair out of her face, she looked around again. "Gamgee," she called, using more force this time. "Gamgee, are you here?"

"Professor Cane." His voice paused between the first and second syllable of doctor, giving the T-sound centre stage. She looked around to find him on the southern walkway.

"Good day," he prompted, brows rising over his thick glasses while he dipped his chin.

"Hey."

He led the way down to the lab floor where he began to make coffee. Gamgee held up the cup and raised his brows again in question. "Sure," Cassidy agreed.

"What brings you to my little operation, Professor

Cane?" he asked, pouring her a cup and handing it over.

"Well, I was in the neighbourhood…" she trailed off, waiting to see his reaction.

Gamgee smirked as he rose to his feet and walked past her to his workstation, resting a hand on the back of the chair. "I'm not the kind of guy who gets a lot of idle visitors," he told her, raising his cup to his mouth, breathing in the aroma of the brew, "and I think I know you well enough to say that you're not the kind of woman to make such idle visits."

"Oh, well," Cassidy shuffled her feet, scuffing one of her boots on the floor.

"I don't have a disaster to fix right now, Professor Cane."

"Come on, Doc!" she burst out. "It's been ages."

He took a sip of his coffee, putting it aside, "Junkie."

"That's why you picked me for this whole business in the first place, right?" she challenged him, gingerly taking up her own cup. Just because she was itching for adventure didn't mean her mind had dulled any, and her wit remained just as sharp.

Gamgee chuckled, "Maybe."

"We both know it is, Doc." Her gaze hardened. "Come on. I saw your map. There are so many places to go. There has to be something you've been working on with them."

"That's classified." He sniffed, walking away from the console.

"Doc, what if you couldn't tinker? What if someone locked you out of all the labs?"

He paused. "Come now, Professor Cane, it isn't all that bad," he said, rubbing some dust off his white coat.

"Just think about it." She pushed further. "Gives you a little itch, doesn't it?"

He raised his eyes to look at her, searching for sensibility. She held his gaze, determined not to back down.

"Well that's because I'm a junkie."

"Come on, Doc!" she reiterated, taking the reins and marching up to the console. She reached for some of the buttons to search for an interesting case on her own.

The doctor's hand snatched one of her wrists away. He was faster than she thought, and stronger than he looked. His actions caught her off guard. She looked to him with surprise. His expression was already falling into a smile though. "Please don't touch the merchandise, Professor Cane." He stepped around her to begin typing for her. "If you're so gung-ho on another operation through the slipstream portals…"

She waited with bated breath, but only got passing minutes of keystrokes until she couldn't hold her breath anymore. "I am." She leaned in, laying her cup near his own discarded drink.

"There was this one portal I've been looking into, but—"

"I'll take it," she declared, already feeling her blood bubbling with anticipation.

"Now hang on," he begged. "This world isn't safe. Despite my belief that this artifact could have a number of uses for us, I've been hesitant to even mention it," he warned.

"Are you starting to doubt me, Doc?" she teased, but also defended herself, hands on hips.

"That's not it. No. I just want you to listen to me. You

must be very careful in this world. It's an extremely dangerous place, and if you don't keep your guard up, then I'll have more troubles than a missing artifact to deal with. Okay?"

"Just give me what you know, and I promise to take any precautions I can."

He hesitated at the console, looking her over with concern once more. His hand drifted left on his three-dimensional model of the earth. She widened her stance and squared her shoulders, exuding as much assurance as she could until he sighed. His hand switched direction and clicked on a portal icon. He typed in his password and released his digital file to Cassidy's email. Her phone beeped in gratitude.

She pulled it out to read what the objective was. "The Lord Stone, huh?" She couldn't help but smirk, "I'm on it."

CHAPTER THREE

Cassidy read her phone as her plane flew over Nebraska. The new portal was almost directly across the country from Plainsfield, Massachusetts. She was heading for the state of Washington, all the way to the Olympic National Park. Once upon a time she had almost hiked the Pacific trail, but had chosen an assistant position on an anthropological study instead. If this portal didn't do enough to get her blood pumping, then she decided that she might just take some time to hike part of the trail.

The commercial plane touched down at the Seattle-Tacoma International Airport. Cassidy went through the motions of disembarking. None of it put her off. Travel was her life, and plane rides were the most mundane part of her travels. She quickly collected her gear and headed for a rental company. While a ferry ride might be more fun, she figured she might as well enjoy driving a car and the climate controls it offered while she could. The file warned her that she would be technologically advanced to the native citizens of this portal world. That meant leaving her phone behind.

As she drove toward the mountain range, she went over the file in her mind. Gamgee called the world Ohkshhon. The inhabitants, the Ohks, were likened to East Asian warriors. They were in a similar situation to the feudal era or middle ages period. So, she decided she would choose her hiking boots in preparation for having to ride horseback.

She arrived at the Olympic National park – making good time - and got everything settled away for the car before she had a small brunch. Then it was time to set out on the trail.

Cassidy walked the path where it was crowded, but took her time to let the majority of her fellow hikers break away from her. She lagged as much as she could, knowing she would soon have to stray from the marked trail. She found a stream that had been noted in the file and followed it downhill. When she came to where it turned back east, she saw a tree with white painted bark. That was her signal to turn west. Hiking over the next hill and back down again left her with sweat soaking the sides of her head. It wasn't uncomfortable to her though. Rather, the sweat of a hard trek served to give her a nostalgic feeling. It also gave her the expectation of an adventure on the horizon.

Speaking of adventures, she reminded herself, she had to keep her eyes open for the next part. The portal was positioned where the trees were older and much larger. They soon became so large that they were open on the bottom, roots supporting them even though the ground had fallen away over years of erosion. Or one could look at it as the trees raising up, able to stand on their own merits, confident in their own strength.

Cassidy closed her compass when she arrived at the tree grown so far from the earth that it looked like an archway to the kingdom of the forest. Just to be sure, she checked her GPS. She was in the right spot. However, to be absolutely one hundred percent sure, Cassidy took off her hiking pack and lay down on the soft earth. She shifted until she had the right angle on the light. She leaned to one side to see the light beaming around the trunk of the tree, and then the other, seeing much the same. Then she focused on the archway. Just as Gamgee had said, the light was wrong. What little light got through bent wrong. It was coloured differently, too. A purple hue in spite of the bright day around her.

"You're definitely the portal," Cassidy concluded, hopping up onto her feet, brushing damp dirt off her jacket. She grabbed her pack and took a new breath, walking up to the archway, sizing up the opening. She had a foot of clearance over her head, so no worries there. Taking a step back, she readied herself, rehearsing her plan over in her head again.

Three...Two...One...

***

Cassidy tensed as she passed through the portal, concentrating on the task of breathing out. She had decided that it would be best to be ready when she landed in a new world. 'Always be ready to run,' was the motto that played through her mind more with each portal excursion. If she started at a run, she could have the advantage of surprise over the native denizens.

She felt fresh ground under her boots and started into a sprint before her new surroundings became entirely clear. Luckily, her other senses were quicker than her head. She came to an abrupt stop as quickly as she had set off. Her muscles tensed over and over, wanting to move forward, but before she could question why she wasn't moving, the rest of those senses caught up. She found her nose was just shy of a short stone obelisk. She had almost run headlong into a sculpted rock! So it looked to her that she would have to rethink her entrance strategy again.

There were locals in the area too. They jumped into action once they swallowed their surprise, just seconds short of her senses coming back to life. So much for getting away. They were in close quarters, and it was dark.

"Careful!" One put out his arm, wrapping it around her front.

"Vaso!" another hissed in criticism. But was that a criticism of her, or the man leading her a step back from her near collision?

"It's fine," the man replied. "Go and tell them the promise has been delivered."

The sound of quickened footsteps upon stone soon dissipated.

"Vaso, be careful," the other warned again, sounding as if he felt she was some viper that could lash out at them without warning.

"We're fine, Qui," Vaso insisted confidently.

It took her a few extra seconds to follow the conversation. It wasn't English, but it wasn't indecipherable, either. Judging by their tones, she was able to guess at the roots of their phonology. The language was very close to modern Mandarin. When she looked at the one called Vaso, Cassidy saw he had every reason to be calm and confident. He was decked out in armour and belted with more than one weapon.

If she were to guess a comparison, she'd say the world of Ohkshhon was definitely in a time similar to the Middle Ages, except a little more fantastical. While he appeared to have all the layers of garb, his armour was far from a full suit. The only plates she could see were on his shoulders and forearms.

That's when Cassidy realized how fantastical this world she had arrived in truly was. Vaso was holding fire. In his other hand was no torch, no lantern, but just fire.

"What is it, Promised One?" his mouth twitched with amusement in response to her uncomfortable expression.

"The name's Cassidy. Cassidy Cane. And I'm alright on my own, thanks. No chance of crashing into any of the statuary," she said, testing out her interpretation of their tongue. His brow scrunched a little, but he definitely understood her. She directed his arm away from her, but her gaze continued to linger on the open flame in his hand. Although he held it safely away from her, it was still unsettling.

She pulled her focus back to take in more of their surroundings. Since she appeared to have found herself among peaceful inhabitants, or at least those who were peaceful towards her, Cassidy couldn't help but look around her to take in clues about the culture she had landed in. It felt like they were underground. The room was damp, and old by the look of the stonework. She even saw some cobwebs catching the flicker of light from

Vaso's hand.

A man, dressed similar to Vaso and Qui, came down the path, holding a lamp aloft to illuminate the way. He was leading a woman to them. She was tall, and strong looking with the width of her shoulders. Her raven hair was loose and damp, clinging to her breastplate. She wore a dark sash draped from shoulder to hip. Cassidy guessed that this represented a station of importance that the woman held. That and the fact that Vaso stepped aside to allow her a full view of Cassidy. He shifted to hold the flame in his hand upward in order to help illuminate Cassidy better. Both women inspected one another.

The woman's dark eyes narrowed upon Cassidy. "Where is your weapon?"

"I don't need one. Usually," Cassidy declared.

The woman's expression made it clear that she didn't entirely believe that.

"What sort of protection is this?" she tapped the back of her hand against Cassidy's jacket.

"I like to think I'm fast enough without all that metal," Cassidy hit back with quick words.

The woman snorted, "You speak so strange."

Cassidy could only respond with a shrug to that one. At least they *could* speak to one another.

"Honoured Guardian," Vaso urged, but he earned himself a harsher glance from her.

She took in a stiff breath through her nose, staying focused on Cassidy, "I am called Saka. The prince's safety is my sole purpose."

Cassidy hesitated over this fresh bundle of information. They seemed to expect that she knew more about them than she actually did.

Vaso gasped, waving his hand. The flames fell to the floor in cinders where they fizzled and extinguished. "Demon's tongue." He growled into the darkness.

The unnamed man came forward to illuminate their circle with his lantern. Saka took the light from him. "What are you called?" she asked.

Cassidy's eyes drifted to Vaso who was carefully trying to remove his charred glove. "Is he alright?"

"Your name. **Now**," Saka demanded. The flame within the lamp flickered wildly as if in response to her impatience.

"Sorry. My name's Cassidy. Cassidy Cane."

"Cane." Saka breathed, exchanging a look with her peers. "Take her bag. Let's get back to the fresh air." She waved and then took the lead once Cassidy had surrendered her pack.

CHAPTER FOUR

They came out into a land of grassy hills with the odd stone jutting out like they had long ago been dropped by giants. The path worn into the grass led further on toward a wood. Just aside from the entrance of the wood sat a group in similar Middle Ages armour. Saka trotted up to a rather large and well-kept man. Cassidy thought that must be the prince.

"Ohto." She bowed her head, "The one of Cane is here."

"Finally," a different man replied. Maybe not a man, though. He looked no older than a teenager. As he rose to his feet, everyone around him immediately bowed their heads in reverence. He paused to re-assess his guard's expression. "What is it, Saka?"

"She is far from expected," she muttered.

He leaned out around her shoulder to look at Cassidy with bright but sunken eyes. "Ah. But she is what was promised," he declared.

Cassidy couldn't help but worry about the boy. He looked like his armour was weighing him down, and it wasn't even as extensive an outfit as those who were with him.

"Promised by who exactly?" she pondered out loud.

Saka turned upon her, eyes aflame with insult, "Do not speak out of turn."

"It's fine, Saka." Ohto sounded exhausted by the few words. "Your coming was foreseen."

"Huh." Cassidy's mind raced around the ideas of what that could mean. Was there an actual seer imbibing hallucinogens? Or a really vague legend from ages past? Or maybe it was a shaman who was rather adept at reading people, like modern fortune tellers?

Then again, with the slipstream portal, there was also the chance that others had been here before. Possibly even Dr. Gamgee. No doubt any visitor would not be as cognizant of their difference in technology before arrival. So, legends of all manner could quickly form around this area.

"Honoured Guardian." The larger guard that she had mistaken as the prince interrupted. His face was showing markings that Cassidy was sure hadn't been there before. The marks were glowing from under his skin.

"Guard, form up!" Saka barked, pushing in closer to the prince.

"Any sense of what to expect, Biren?" Vaso asked, sword in hand.

"Not yet."

Suddenly, the ground erupted in white flame. It travelled in a line like it was following gunpowder that had been laid down and aimed right for Cassidy. Vaso jammed his sword into the earth before the fire could reach them.

When it met his blade, they heard a crash. The energy visibly dissipated. Cassidy felt it push through her hair as it passed over them like warm winds of the west coast. Qui thrust his hands upward, spreading a dust which took form over their heads. He had done so just in time. A projectile met the form and exploded like fireworks, leaving a shower of static that fizzled along Qui's barrier. The sparks that hit the ground outside of their safety field burned the grass and blackened the soil.

"It's Ghost People," the big glowing guy, Biren, announced.

"I think we can *see* that." Vaso grunted, pulling his sword free from the ground to then parry the blade of an enemy who had attacked at a running pace. The whitest creature Cassidy had ever seen had rushed through their protective barrier to attack with force. Her brilliant blade was aimed for the prince. The woman's hair and skin were as white as milk, while her eyes were impossibly dark. It brought to mind the representation of demonic possession in some horror movie she'd seen once.

"Eyes on the other two," Saka commanded.

"Right, there's always three," Biren thought out loud, scanning around their group.

Cassidy looked around them. It wasn't like she could be of much help otherwise. Truthfully, she could hardly keep up with everything going on around her. It was enough just to push her beliefs to agree with what her eyes took in. Suspending disbelief in a theoretical study was one thing, but when the impossible was happening all around her, it seemed to make her head spin.

"Shimmer. There!" Qui pointed. With his other hand,

he appeared to be rolling something across the ground. Smoke shot out of the soil like a geyser. Within the steam were two pale women. The first one had her hair and garments loose. She waved one palm over the other and grew a ghostly flame between them. She made a witch-like silhouette with her cape fluttering, black as night around her. Meanwhile, the second, who had tightly braided lengths of white hair and more fitted clothing, charged toward them, drawing a set of peculiar blades. The same ghostly flame the witch summoned began to flicker down the curved lengths of her twin swords.

Oh no, Cassidy thought, seeing that she was in the line of fire.

Vaso had pushed the larger ghost woman away from their group while Qui was busy sending volleys at their two new foes, forcing the second woman off her course and then to retreat a few steps.

Cassidy drifted back to Saka and the prince. "You have a plan?"

Saka was about to answer but Ohto touched her wrist and she closed her mouth. "They are pressing us toward the wood."

"A trap?" she asked.

"Most likely."

"Do you have a counter?"

"Only faith," he replied, a glint in his sunken eyes. "Let's go."

She looked worried, then conceded to his will. "I will cover you as far as I can. Let us try to avoid triggering this trap."

He nodded. "Ready, Cane?"

Cassidy smirked, feeling a rush coming over her. Their group began to edge back, losing ground to their attackers with the wood looming larger and larger. Their big guy was knocked to the ground by the woman with twin blades. She took her chance and leaped toward Ohto and Cassidy. Saka intercepted, catching her by the neck. "Go back to the shade," she shouted, driving her pale foe into the dirt. With a swift kick for good measure, she turned to make a run for it. Ohto did too, grabbing hold of Cassidy's hand, towing her along.

They crossed into the forest, finding it tightly grown and dim. Cassidy could hear her blood beginning to thrum through her veins. The odds of walking into a trap were highly likely. They made it down the path and took a turn before phantom flames cut them off. Saka threw herself in front of them and waved the end of her sash over the surrounding fire, killing most of it. The fabric glowed in her hold, showing there was more to it than expected. "I'll block them here as long as I can."

"Don't overdo it," Ohto begged.

"As you command, my prince." She dug her hand into a pouch. "Go now."

Spreading glowing stones before her in a fluid motion, Saka created a chain reaction of elements. Cassidy didn't get the chance to appreciate the power of this display, though.

Ohto pulled her along as they ran further down the path. They took a fork to a lower and less worn part of the woods. They ran until they were crashing through the brush, speeding downhill, and then they lost traction. They tumbled down in a heap.

"Are you okay?" Cassidy gasped. "Oh." She rubbed her shin, realizing they had run into a line of little standing stones. Ohto looked at his bloody knee, then found a deep gash on his hand. He began to shake.

"Hey. Hey. It's okay. I have clean bandages." Cassidy reached into her pocket. "Can I check the wound?" If they hadn't taken her pack, she could have cleaned it too, but that would have to wait. He gave her his hand without argument.

"Why do you trust me?" she asked, looking to distract him as she dabbed the bloody wound, squinting in the waning light of dusk.

"You are the one who was promised. The answer in Cane," he replied, fully believing that his words made sense.

"Was it a prophecy?"

"Not entirely. I just know," he muttered through the stinging. "I can tell you have a good heart," he said, though he winced again and paled.

Maybe. But not the best of intentions, Cassidy thought to herself.

"Why are they attacking you?" she wondered.

"They want to stop me from being anointed in the capital," he murmured, drawing his gaze downward. "I am heir to the throne, which my father has ascended from."

"They want to destabilize the region?" Cassidy interpreted. He didn't sound too keen when he mentioned this anointment, though.

Noises of battle echoed from up the hill. "We must hurry," Ohto urged, fear coming to his voice.

"All done." Cassidy tied the bandage and sat back

on her heels, looking at their surroundings. "We should probably get away from the path altogether."

"That is a sound plan," he agreed, though his voice grew weaker with each crashing sound that reached their ears.

Cassidy looked at the standing stones they had tripped over, brushing her hand over the carved symbols on the one closest to her. She looked at all the other stones. They were placed in a kind of pattern around her and the prince. The symbols reminded her of native etchings, telling others of safe spaces, good hunting grounds, and of home. Following a similar symbology, she read the stone telling her to look to her right, then the next right, and a left. She followed them until she walked into a piece of a statue. A large head, gawking at them from overgrown shrubbery.

She pulled back the leaves and recoiled from the horrible expression forever contorting the face of stone.

"Whatever's the matter?" Ohto followed her at a distance, then shuddered to find the face as well. "What an awful omen."

Sounds of thunder reached them, followed by lightning strikes flashing in the distance.

"Actually," Cassidy began to ponder to herself, "if I'm right..." She began to press her hands around the stone crevasses of the head, trying the mouth, the eyes, ears, but nothing budged. She felt like she was about to be disappointed.

But far from it, in fact! The challenge posed by this puzzle gave her a nagging sense that she could not let go of. It was a special sort of excitement that seeded within her. With the added pressure of the danger drawing ever closer to them, she was simply, pleasantly, abuzz. Cassidy took her time, walking around the structure. Once she was at the back of the skull, she pressed in and felt the surface give under her force. She tried again and noticed the surface bounce. "I think this could be our way out," she announced, gaining his full attention, though the prince looked aghast at the option she offered.

Another clap of thunder boomed through the forest, and lightning screeched through the air, making Ohto duck in fright. The battles were getting closer.

"How will this help us get away?" He made up his mind, eager to get away safely.

Cassidy smirked, "It's a false back." She dragged her hands down along the superbly crafted seam. Anyone could have mistaken it for a crack placed there by age. Near the ground, she found space for her grip. Taking hold, she lifted the false back to show it was a cleverly disguised hatch that now welcomed them into a hidden path.

"Wow." Ohto breathed. Quickly, he ducked again from the increasing noise of combat. "Can we go?"

"I thought you'd never ask." Cassidy took the lead, ducking under the hatch and descending into the unknown.

***

Once they were inside, the hatch closed behind them and plunged them into darkness.

"Do you have a torch?" Cassidy asked, remembering that her things were still in the care of his guards.

"I have better than that crude solution," he informed

her. She listened to his breathing as it changed in the darkness. First, he gave a directed exhale, then another, but more open this time. Light began to form between them.

"Woah," she exclaimed.

The prince was holding up a faceted crystal. "You have your talents, Cane, and I have mine," he offered with some cheek. Dust fell from overhead, bringing his expression down as well. "Let us move onward."

As they walked along the cobbled underground path, the sounds of battle faded away. Cassidy observed the construction of the path they were on. It was well-made, but had no remarkable images added and no ornaments. The path was only for utility. At least, on this end. So it couldn't hold her interest for very long. Instead, her focus shifted to the crystal. She had a mission here.

"How does it work?" she asked, pointing at the shard that lit their way.

"Be careful! Don't get too close." He shifted to the other side of the path. "Don't you have Vital Stones where you come from?"

"No. Not ones that can do that at least." She paused, "Is it the stone doing that? Or you?"

"I am only the spark. A conduit. Men cannot create what isn't already in the essence of the stone," Ohto recited as though he were recalling text like one of her students in the lecture hall.

"So, it's naturally occurring?"

"That is the basis of it," he murmured.

Cassidy took a moment to ponder the depth of this new information. If the stone held such energy that it could be coaxed to create light, or fire, or lightning, along with any number of feats she had witnessed since coming through the portal, then it was definitely a hazardous material. "Then it must be dangerous to obtain."

"Warrior societies are the only ones who really use it. We hone our knowledge and skill to wield Vital Stones in the service of the people and the Master Kings."

Cassidy's eyes widened.

Ohto laughed bitterly, "You're surprised to learn that even I shall have to answer to another." He huffed again with self-mockery. "Though the warrior societies are few, they are kept in check by those who speak for the majority. Or such was the theory."

Cassidy had so many questions, but she forced herself to stick with what would help her to uncover the artifact she came here for. "There are bigger stones, right? Stronger ones?"

Ohto sighed, "I supposed there is no one who wouldn't know." He glanced at her. "I wonder how much simpler all this could be if such things could remain legend."

"What do you mean?"

"Out of the five kingdoms, ours is said to be the strongest. This is not due to our numbers, but simply because we posses the Lord Stone."

"And that's a big deal?" she chose her words carefully.

"Well the king ascended and now the only one with knowledge and access to the Lord Stone is me. The stone with powers to recharge any Vital Stone, among many other mysteries." He sighed again.

"Wow. It's a very big deal then." She breathed, doing her best not to let on what a relief it was to finally have clues and know that she was on the right path to her objective.

"It makes for a big target." He grumbled. "The kingdom hasn't known a moment's peace since the Lord Stone was uncovered." Ohto sliced the air with his free hand. The light in his other hand dimmed for a moment and then renewed its strength with a surge that was not unlike Edison's bulb.

Cassidy let herself fall behind by a step as a precaution. "I'm sorry," she murmured.

"It's of little consequence now. You are here. And my fortunes are in the wind."

"Come again?" she stopped walking altogether.

"Hm?" Ohto paused. "Oh. Pay me no mind. Just simple musings," he assured her with a gentle smile.

Cassidy felt that whatever his musings might be, they were definitely not simple. He continued on without her but stopped a few feet away. "Ah. I think we are here."

Cassidy jogged to catch up and found that they had come to the end of the path. Before them stood a door with an ornate steel design.

"What do you think?" he asked. "Are we about to interrupt someone's dinner?"

Cassidy looked the door over, noting the caked dust and the undisturbed webbing. "If we are, I'd bet we'd be disturbing the kitchen maid," she joked, lifting the latch and pushing the door open.

CHAPTER FIVE

The sound of the hinges would certainly alert anyone to their intrusion. However, Cassidy soon concluded that they were likely alone. What little provisions that were left in the room were long past rotten. The place had been picked over by smaller creatures and possibly wanderers. She wished she could have seen the architecture better, but Ohto led the way with his light, having no interest in the tight lower quarters of the building.

Together they passed through an archway and found her conclusions to be entirely true. The floor of the main room was rotted and collapsing. The ornate window that overlooked the entire space was broken. Once upon a time it had probably lit the area with brilliance through its coloured glass. One staircase had fallen in at the bottom, leaving the other staircase as the only means to get to the second level. That is, if they wanted to. Cassidy was all for exploring, especially with uncertainty at hand, but Ohto seemed to be a far more cautious person.

As if in spite of her assumptions, he continued to walk ahead of her, leading the way up the stairs. He seemed to be looking for something. She followed him to keep from being swallowed up by the darkness of the space. On the first landing, he paused, holding up his glowing gem to a nearby statue. It had its face smashed off and was missing the end of its outstretched arm below the elbow. She glanced to Ohto who surveyed the statue like a scholar in a museum. She looked back to the statue, noting it was definitely the likeness of a man. His other hand was rested on his chest, like he was pledging to something.

"Nobu," Ohto named him. "The ancestor who almost united the kingdoms."

"What happened?" Cassidy leaned in to try and get a better view of the statue without falling off the landing. There were no obvious crests, only simple leaf motifs embellishing his armour.

"Greed." Ohto murmured, "an inability to close the gaps in our differences." He shifted, casting the light around the landing until he found another statue. This one was of a woman with half her face smashed. Her ears were small and pointed and she even had the same markings down her arm as the Ghost People.

"Tela-Na. Nobu's chosen partner. It caused great scandal." He huffed in amusement, "It scandalizes to this day, though they are but history."

"So, people don't like to mix with those who are different?" This land wasn't so detached from her own, Cassidy thought.

"They don't like what they don't know, and if they have power, those people make laws about what everyone else can ever know."

Cassidy admired the boy. He was incredibly intelligent and perceptive for his age. Heck! Even for his rank. Most that were fortunate enough to be crowned in their youth had a tendency to rest on their laurels; a sad Commodus to the Marcus Aurelius.

The light dimmed, causing Cassidy to look up. It was then that she saw Ohto wiping at his cheek with his free hand.

"Hey, what's wrong?"

He shook his head, making sure to stand straighter. That just made her heart go out to him even more. Like watching JFK Jr. saluting a casket. She took a deep breath, "I'm nobody. I'm not from here, just passing through. So... you can talk to me, whatever you say will be safe."

He looked back at her, trembling as he continued to wipe away tears, sniffling. "Nobu gave up his crown to be with Tela-Na. He did everything to lead the way through his example...and the people followed him, for the most part." He took in a calmer breath before continuing, "My father, the Ascended King, Juto. He was a great man too. He brought the clans of the region together, bartering with feuding clans to establish one of the greatest hubs for our warriors." He took a shaking breath, getting to his point. "I am no leader."

"Why would you say that? Saka and the others seem pretty dedicated to you," she countered.

"I make them fools." He sneered, "They will die for naught."

"Don't say that." She felt her mouth turn down.

"I have no plan, Cassidy. I never do. With all I have, all I could manage back there was buckling to my own wants to run."

He was only a boy. To face such burdens, Cassidy wanted to shake her head. She'd studied different types of monarchs throughout history and while they all coped differently, with varying outcomes, there was never any doubt of the strain such a position placed on them. The hardest for anyone to watch, even through the pages of history, were the young.

"It's normal to be scared." She said, "That was a serious life and death situation back there. There's nothing wrong with being scared in that."

"No."

"You're not a coward," she declared, feeling certain of that. She saw the look in his eye, a mirror of what she knew she held in the face of dangers that promised adventure.

"You misunderstand." He broke her bubble. "It wasn't just the battle that made me want to run. It's all of it. The duty, the relations, the power, everything to do with the Lord Stone."

"Oh."

"It weighs on me like a curse." He breathed, "I didn't want this destiny. And I knew that when they came to me," He reflected.

"You accepted anyway?"

"It wasn't simple. But also, I must admit, I wanted the power. Some of it at least. Just not the bulk of it." He sighed, "But you can't break it apart." He mused.

Cassidy stayed quiet for a couple minutes, going over the situation in full. What he said did nothing to change how she felt about him, but she felt it would be rude if she couldn't control her elation. He had just shown her an opening, the chance to make this mission easier. Plus, while she didn't mind a challenge, war zones were a whole other story. Gamgee had been right in his assessment of this world. It was mortally dangerous.

"Well, what if you could get rid of it?"

"What?" he demanded.

She was surprised to find her pulse quickening, but continued speaking, or perhaps her increasing adrenaline was why she did. "What if I took it away? No Lord Stone, no feuds," she offered. "Maybe then you might be able to step back from all the pressures, at least until you're ready for all of the duties," she declared sagely.

His eyes shifted away as he pondered her offer.

She turned her head to look out into the darkened sky. A falling star appeared. The drifting spark caught Ohto's gaze as well. Cassidy cocked her head to the side, focusing harder. The star looked odd. She watched for a couple more seconds before she figured it out.

It was falling toward them.

"Get down!" Ohto cried, shoving her to the side as he dove away. She hit the floor hard, but that didn't matter. They were overtaken by the sound of something crashing through the rest of the glass. The 'star' exploded in the centre of the landing. Cassidy was thrown back further, catching herself on the pillar by the old stairs.

Scrambling upright, her eyes darted about in search of the prince. She strained to see through the darkness and the dust. Then her gaze focused on movement at the epicentre of the explosion. Steam continued to roll out from the spot where a man now stood. Markings on his arm glowed painfully bright. That was when she realized that it wasn't dust or steam, it was fog. The Ghost People had found them.

CHAPTER SIX

Ohto straightened himself up, taking his time. His foe watched, unmoving.

It was hard to hear the prince. The air crackled while the entire structure was still settling from the disruptive intrusion.

"I don't want this," Ohto murmured, hesitating over his next move.

The Ghost Man lifted his arm. The mist came to life, forming a stream that raced toward the prince. Ohto took the blow, stumbling to the side. With a turn of his wrist, the Ghost Man brought the stream back around, knocking Ohto in the other direction.

Using both hands, he directed the stream to split and come at Ohto from both sides. It raced so fast that Cassidy winced at the thought of the strike.

But the prince caught it this time. When the streams met his hands, they ignited into clouds of fire. Cassidy shielded her face while the area illuminated among the blaze. The heat hissed through the air around them.

The Ghost Man was unmoved though. His eyes widened, but that was all.

Cassidy thought he might yield.

There was no such luck.

"What have you done with it?"

Ohto jumped forward, taking a chance to attack. He unsheathed his blade, diving straight into the man's chest. However, Ohto only tumbled to the floor behind him, rolling onto his knees. Resting his sword down on the floor, the prince frowned. "What is this?"

"A message, boy."

The Ghost Man wasn't really here. He stood before them like a hologram.

Then he captured Cassidy in his dark gaze, eyes piercing the darkness and the fog. "You've brought a Streamer into this?"

Cassidy managed to tear her eyes away from his to look at Ohto. No one had mentioned that they understood Slipstreamers before.

"This world has no need for their kind." The Ghost Man growled, throwing his hand down in her direction. Cassidy flinched out of instinct, even though she knew he wasn't physically here, and the fighting seemed to have come to a halt.

"You're wrong." Ohto got back to his feet, returning his sword to its sheath.

"What do you plan on doing, boy?"

Ohto refused to answer.

He shook his head, chuckling. "Then take your message and see what your Streamer can do."

Ohto glared, crossing his arms in waiting.

"Bring the stone and your men might survive."

"What?"

"Follow the beacon. Then maybe we can put this to rest." He held up the black sash Saka had worn.

Ohto's frustration boiled over quickly. He yelled, thrusting his hand into the ethereal image of his foe, burning off all the fog in a single blast.

The image of his foe evaporated. A wave of heat ran through the air, making the space humid like she was back on the Pacific trail in Washington.

The prince fell to his knees with a groan.

"Ohto," she dashed to his side.

He was shaking all over by the time she placed her hands on his back. She thought he was crying, until the shaking became worse. He dropped to the centre of the blast scar in the clutches of a seizure.

"Oh crap." She knelt, pushing her legs and hands under his head. "Did that creep do this?" she asked no one, counting the seconds as she squinted over him in the darkness.

She hadn't counted very far before he settled down, although it felt like it could have been ten times longer.

"Take it easy." She rested one hand upon his arm.

He groaned.

"How do you feel?"

"Tired," he murmured.

Unfortunately, Ohto's last blast had been powerful enough to destabilize the building.

The landing careened under them.

"We have to go," she cried, pulling him up awkwardly. Somehow, they stumbled down the stairs and out of the crumbling building. As they escaped, she looked back to

see that the entire front of the structure had let go and col-
lapsed. The trees out front were blackened as well. They
looked like they had been caught in a flash fire, burned
to a crisp and left with nothing to feed flame. Some of the
trees even crumbled as they ran by.

They came to a stop a short distance away, catching
their breath. The cold began to set in now that they were
away from the range of the magical fire.

"You said this was about your crown." Cassidy led into
the heart of her discovery. That encounter, while threatening, had given her more truth than these Ohks had.

"It is. The stone is part of my responsibility. We are
not supposed to talk about it."

"Why?"

"Because it corrupts." He stamped his foot into the
hardened soil. "My father's ascension was not by his
choosing."

Cassidy began to wonder what exactly they meant by
that phrase. At first, she thought it was her slip of trans-
lation, a mistake due to a difference in dialect, but they
seemed rather intentional with the words and order they
chose. "When you say ascended," she began to ask.

"He died, mortally." He began to pace, "A living god
ascends to his full power when he completes his mortal
journey."

She blinked, curiosity igniting her mind with this new
information. This culture was becoming increasingly fas-
cinating.

"But the Lord Juto didn't choose to complete his journey so soon. They murdered him."

"The Ghost People?"

"No. The men he trusted. His government of the people. They killed him for want of the stone. They think they'll have it too, holding the kingdom for me, thinking we don't know any better."

"Won't they kill you too, when you arrive? Why weren't they arrested?"

"Plans for my banners are in place. Saka will bring order, and we will establish new governance."

What a mess she had run herself into, Cassidy thought.

"I need her." He kicked the ground, unsettling a tuft of dry grass.

Cassidy raised her chin, looking over the next tree line.

"You're insulted by my failures?"

"Huh. No. I don't see that at all," she argued. "But I do see how you're going to get your guards back." She pointed to the twin of the star that had fallen. "He said follow the beacon, right?"

He returned to her side to check for himself. "That's exactly it." He nodded, then took her hands. "I know I was not entirely forthcoming with the state of our nations. But I do agree with your previous solution. Help me to save them, and the stone will be yours to take from this world."

She wasn't sure how she could help these people, but how could she refuse the offer?

"Deal."

***

They started their hike as thunder began to roll in the atmosphere. The environment had begun working to balance itself again. Cassidy felt a chill the closer they got to the location of the beacon. The journey took a few hours, but the forest was so thick, daylight never reached them. Cassidy paused to take a drink, fixing her red locks back behind her ears. She shrugged her shoulders against the cold and dampness that clung to her. "So, this is probably a trap, right?"

"Hm?" Ohto raised his head from his waterskin. "I expect no less."

"But you only have one plan?"

"For you." He nodded. "With you as a distraction, Saka can choose the best course of action," he said, taking a short sip of water.

"Fine." She glanced back to the beacon, noting this was their last rest before they reached the location under the false star.

Ohto set a faster pace this time, marching hard toward their foes.

Cassidy pushed through wet branches, careful not to slip on the moss beneath her feet. "Hang on."

"We're almost there." Ohto pushed, hesitating in his step.

"Yeah but look." She waved her hand through the air, her skin picking up water droplets from the air around them. "Isn't this their modus operandi?"

"Excuse me?" he frowned at her.

"Oh, uhm. Their usual methods?" she held her hands up on either side of her.

"Yes," he agreed.

Cassidy thought back to the encounter with the phantom image and how the fog had hit the prince. "What if we're ambushed? Maybe we could look for a way around this?"

Ohto opened his mouth to answer, looking tired, but someone else spoke for him.

"No, dear thing, you're already in it."

Ohto looked at her, the colour draining from his face as the fog collected around them, growing dense.

"Where is the stone?" The witchy woman appeared from the murky fogs.

"It's nice of you to ask," Cassidy thought out loud, "but does that ever really work?"

She frowned at Cassidy before taking a bolt to the side. Cassidy smiled, seeing that her distraction had worked, letting Ohto land an attack.

He almost grinned but didn't get the chance.

"It wasn't a question." She crooned, holding her side as the other two stepped from the fog. "It was a command."

She summoned a white fire, throwing it down at Ohto's feet. "You will tell me," she commanded, waving her hand.

Ohto readied a defence but eased up when no attack came.

Instead, her sisters dragged their captives out of the fog. They tossed their prisoners onto the ground before Ohto and Cassidy.

Vaso, Qui, Biren, and Saka. None of them looked ready to take up the fight.

"Saka." Ohto ran toward her. White fire torpedoed between them, cutting off his path to his trusted guards.

"Tell us where you hid the stone," the witch demanded again.

Ohto hesitated. "Saka. Please say something."

Cassidy looked from her allies to their enemies. Maybe she should have pushed for more of a plan. He had seemed so sure in the abilities of his guards. He never thought that they could be too roughed up to mount a counter attack.

"Saka," Ohto begged.

"Ohto, remember who you are." Saka coughed from the dirt.

"What?" Cassidy wondered.

"You don't need to say anything to them," she insisted to the prince.

"Shut up," the witch barked.

But Saka continued, "You never have to say anything to anyone."

"Saka, I can't," he argued.

Cassidy's brows scrunched together, wondering what on earth they were talking about.

"But you can!" she insisted.

"Stop talking." The witch stepped forward, taking Saka by the arm, lifting her off the ground and pressing a palm full of fire to her forearm.

Saka screamed, though Cassidy could tell she was trying to resist the primal urge to show pain. She gritted her teeth, cringing at the sight.

"Do it!" Saka cried with what little breath she had left.

"Enough." The witch took hold of the back of Saka's head. "Kill them all."

Her sisters brandished weapons above their captives.

The men did their best to face down death with courage. Cassidy knew she wanted to look away but, at the same time, couldn't deny their show of honour. Then there was a new sister who took Cassidy's arms behind her back. She got the feeling she wouldn't be included in the execution order. Somehow that made her feel worse.

Something hit the ground, making her look back at the prince, fearing he might be hurt, or worse, having another seizure. All she got was an eyeful of head-splitting bright light.

"What?" the witch screamed.

Cassidy could feel so many things that her mind was quickly overcome. She watched as the witch's arms lit up; all the markings that she had used to craft her spells with were now causing her pain. At least, Cassidy interpreted the contortion of her expression as such. She couldn't hear anything anymore.

She continued to watch as the markings on the witch's arms began to spread, the light bleeding out and pooling together. It looked as though she might be consumed by the power entirely.

Then, Cassidy began to hear again. She heard the strangled breathing of the witch as her knees hit the ground. She heard something else hit the ground behind her again. This time the prince was down. He was on his hands and knees.

And that was all Cassidy could grasp as she was overcome with the pain in her head.

CHAPTER SEVEN

"You did well."

Cassidy gasped for air as she came to. She sat up on instinct, but the swirling in her head protested the act. She rested the side of her head in her hand, blinking to gain better sight of her surroundings.

Saka was sitting nearby. She nodded toward Cassidy upon noting she had awakened.

Ohto turned to face her, "You're awake."

"Seems like it," she mumbled, rubbing her head lightly. She was still seeing stars behind her eyes.

"I'm sorry you were caught in that." He leaned in closer to her. She still felt woozy, like they were moving, or swaying a little.

"It's fine. Nothing broken, I think." She checked her arms and hands, then looking down at her legs. Her pants were dirty and scuffed in the knees, but everything was intact.

"I cannot apologize enough." Ohto bowed his head.

Saka glared at him, leaning her head in close as well. "You finally showed them a taste of what they get by attacking our people."

Ohto visibly deflated.

"If only you allowed your conviction to shine through. Then you would truly have shown them the might that we hold," Saka insisted.

Cassidy glanced to the prince. He clearly didn't like those words. He looked physically weighed down all over again.

"What's going on?" Cassidy finally realized they really were moving. All of them. She looked past the others and noted canvas walls and a roof over them. It flapped, dulling the sounds of nature beyond. They were in a covered wagon. She could hear the wheels grinding along the terrain, and they bumped around painfully.

"I failed," Ohto murmured, dipping his chin.

"You did very well. Next time you will succeed," Saka assured him. She hadn't given up in her push to sculpt him into a warrior more like herself.

"We have been captured!" Ohto argued, throwing his hands down in frustration.

"Yeah. It seems the end is coming closer," Vaso insisted. He was seated in the corner close to the driver box beyond the wall. His hands were bound, though his leg appeared to be burned on top of the bruises and contusions he had suffered in battle.

There were too many holes in her knowledge. It didn't feel like Cassidy had been hit in the head. She just felt groggy. Questions raced into her mind, but she took a moment to sort them. Qui was not among them but she felt that she knew the worst had come to him in their last encounter. Why would they not have brought him, otherwise? The most appropriate question seemed to be: "How? How were we captured?"

"I overpowered their magic," Ohto admitted gravely. "Only, we all got caught up in it."

"I see." That didn't answer her question in the way she had wanted.

"They prevailed through the attack this time." Saka sat back with confidence, "Next time they won't be so lucky."

"Saka." He fretted.

"They're taking us to our deaths!" Vaso argued with her.

"You should trust me," she snapped back at him. "Or rather, you should trust in our prince."

Ohto shifted uncomfortably.

"They demanded the stone. He is leading them to the border." She smiled.

"That's where you called your banners to meet you, right?" Cassidy thought out loud. "Before you were marching on the city."

"Precisely. Even this foolish Streamer sees the plan." Saka cocked her thumb in Cassidy's direction.

Cassidy looked to Ohto instead of letting the guard see her insecurity with the presented prospect.

"Cane," he leaned over to take one of her hands in his. "Your coming was not coincidence. You are meant to help us."

"Uh..." She looked down to avoid everyone's eyes. His hands felt so bony.

"I think you were right. You can help with this burden. You can free this land of its curse." He gripped her hand firmly. His bones kind of hurt. But his intention was made clear. He still wanted her to take the stone.

The plan did make sense. With all his men gathered at the border, their captors would be outnumbered, and quickly overpowered. Then he could give her the stone and be on his way to the capital to win his throne. So, there wouldn't be much to worry about. She could sit back and let it play out. Yet Cassidy no longer felt very good about that fact. Of course, she thought to herself in an attempt to shrug it off, this would be an utterly boring conclusion to her trip.

***

They bumped along for a while. On Saka's orders everyone rested in relative silence. When the wagon finally jerked to a stop, they all perked up, stretching a little while they waited to be let out. But no one opened the gate on the back of the wagon. No one came for them.

"What are you doing here?" the witch's voice demanded from the driver's box.

"You thought you could leave me behind, Sister Noh?"

"My sisters have done the bulk of the work in securing the stone. I'd rather be drained by the shadow before I let you take the credit, Pun-ni."

Cassidy perked up. The voice was from the man that had given them the ultimatum. Only now did Cassidy realize that he had been absent from their rendezvous at the beacon. It sounded to her like that hadn't been his choice, though.

"It is not about credit, Sister Noh. We have a duty."

"A mission to get the stone, we are all very much aware of that," she growled out her annoyance. "Now get out of the way."

"You are mistaken, Sister."

"Shut up and get out of the way." Another sister rocked the wagon with her movement. Probably the larger one.

Silence passed over them all.

"So be it. Run him over," Noh ordered.

They clattered forward once more.

"That's right. Stay off the road, Pun-ni, if you know what's good for you."

The group in the back exchanged looks with one another, but no one saw fit to comment. Cassidy looked to each of them, until her eyes were caught by the prince. His eyes shifted from side to side, lines creasing around his mouth and into his forehead with the force of his thoughts.

She wondered what he might have perceived from the encounter. She wondered if the schism among the Ghost People might prove to be a benefit to them in the coming surprise they were approaching. There would be no telling until they arrived.

***

The wagon drove for hours more. There had been a couple stops for their captors to check on them and give them water. Cassidy stayed awake throughout the entire journey, while the others dozed. She couldn't get comfortable in this situation. Although she was sure a way out would present itself sooner or later.

"How much longer?" Vaso mumbled to Saka.

"Not long. They'll probably drive right into our legions." She smiled over the thought.

Biren, their larger guard, shifted on his seat, grunting his discomfort.

Eventually, Saka leaned over and nudged Ohto awake, "It's almost time."

He nodded, drawing himself up to sit as if he wanted to make himself smaller.

***

They arrived at last. All of them were led off the wagon and into the strong winds coming through the valley. Cassidy looked at the cliffs looming overhead, and the mountain at the end of the road.

"There is an old structure up this mountain." Ohto gestured his hands toward it, not missing a beat in finding the road completely abandoned.

"We know." The witch muttered, pushing him ahead of her.

The way up was steep. The red silt where there wasn't slate was very loose. Even the Ghost People stumbled from time to time. Soon they came to steps hastily driven into the mountainside. Ohto continued, though sweat had stuck his hair flat to his head.

He looked ready to collapse by the time they saw the top. The slate rock had grown up around them, the steps twisting, having been cut into the stone itself. The way was pitted, but at least it was stable. Their captors ushered them to the final landing.

One storey below them Cassidy could see an unexpected temple laid out.

"Huh." Cassidy looked around at the carved pillars

that held nothing up, and the markings on the walls that remained. It was more like an open amphitheatre, perhaps. This wasn't unlike the Parthenon of Athens, albeit it was adorned with the remnants of Ohks symbology and colours. The pillars had been washed dark, and red sand was running along the floor, laid down in designs. She wondered what it would look like from a higher vantage point.

Saka huffed, garnering a shove from the larger sister.

They descended in single file. Though the walls protected them, the sound of the wind was still fierce. It made this place feel even more desolate and detached from the world. It was probably how so many warriors were able to elude their notice though. At least, until it was too late. The warriors collected to fight for Ohto marched out and surrounded them once their group hopped off the last steps.

The sisters looked from the soldiers to their captives while Cassidy basked in elation. There was nothing quite like the figurative cavalry to move your heart to thanks. Not quite the right buzz, but she'd let it slide this time.

Saka shoved the witch, Noh, out of the way to keep her from grabbing at the prince in desperation.

The other sisters brandished their swords.

"You can't be serious." Vaso gaped at them, "You're outnumbered."

"It's actually not that simple," Biren stated, stepping forward from the back of the group to join the sisters. The shorter one cut the ties off his hands. At the same time, many of the soldiers attacked their own men.

"What?" Saka cried out, looking around them in disbelief.

Ohto took a step closer to Cassidy.

"We knew what would be waiting here all along," Noh told them, ignoring the battle that broke out before them.

"It's too bad our main informant perished in the last encounter, but Biren will just have to manage with double the payment." She smiled to him, and his face broke into a grin as he accepted a blade from the larger sister.

"How dare you." Saka sneered as she ducked under his first hearty slash.

Noh zeroed in on Ohto and Cassidy.

"If I were to guess, I'd say they took your magic Vital Stones away?" Cassidy shuffled back one pace, only to hop aside as a pair of soldiers tumbled through.

"Something like that," Ohto stuttered.

"I'll ask one more time, boy. Where have you placed the stone?" Noh stalked toward them. Her movement reminded Cassidy of a cat on the prowl. Ohto grabbed Cassidy's arm and pulled her back. To her surprise, Cassidy saw the witch pull away too. She jumped quite like that proverbial cat, caught off guard by a wall of fire erupting between them. More to the point, it was white fire.

"This is going too far, Sister Noh." Pun-ni rushed in, placing himself in front of the prince.

"You are depraved." She laughed. "I told you to stay away. And yet you insist on blocking our victories with your twisted beliefs? You need recognition that badly?" She waited, but he did not stand down. "Then you'll suffer the consequences."

"Sister Noh, yield now. We can take care of this together without bloodshed," he said, attempting to appeal to logic.

"You think you can stand up to all this?" she waved her hands wide, encompassing the growing battle. She definitely had more on her side now. The surprise betrayal had reduced the number of Ohto's men before they could even act. With the balance of numbers shifted from the outset it seemed likely that they would soon be entirely defeated.

Pun-ni turned his head to the side, then back to Noh. "I will have to try." His arms ignited, fog billowing from him, gathering and forming into the shape of men, interrupting the final slaughter and pushing back their foes.

"Take this and run." Pun-ni held out a knife. Cassidy took it, using it to free Ohto's hands and then letting him free her.

The prince took her hand and dragged her around the battles until they found a room that was cut into the mountain wall.

Cassidy saw the statues that stood over rows of sarcophagi. Each with its own stone to light their faces and the space itself. Her stomach dropped. They were in a crypt. The prince didn't seem to care as he led her to the end of the row, hiding behind the largest statue.

"Ohto, what are you doing?"

"I can't. Last time I burned up their magic, I...no. I won't do it."

"Okay, then let's protect the stone," Cassidy offered.

He shook his head, "It might be best to destroy it. You see how it twisted that woman? How greed has seeped into my own trusted guards, ones I would have called friends. My own sworn swords are tearing each other apart for its power."

"Where is it, Ohto?" she demanded in desperation. If she could grab it and get away before he smashed it, then things might work out. Or so she told herself weakly.

"Very close."

"You mean it's in here?" she turned to try and see him in the dim light of the room.

"Yes."

A thud shook the space, dust rushing over them.

"I have to show you," Ohto insisted.

"What? We have to be quick. This is a dead end," Cassidy countered, looking from him to the billowing dust coming in from the only way out. Or more likely, it was the fog of the Ghost People.

Ohto grabbed her hand. Cassidy tried to pull away out of instinct. "What are we doing?" she looked at him, but his grip only tightened, bones digging in, adding to the tension.

"Quickly," he hissed. "You need to understand. You must take it!" he pressed her hand into his chest, along the lower ribs. He exhaled completely, and her eyes widened.

What is that?

Something was under the skin. Something that shouldn't be there. A foreign object. Her eyes widened again, and she gasped, not wanting to believe it was true.

"Yes," he said lowly and nodding. "Take it quickly, before they get here. Break it on first strike if you must. Save us all from this curse."

She strained her eyes to glance back at the entrance. Crashes echoed down the path and throughout the crypt.

Enemies and traitors alike were working to get to them, to capture prince Ohto. How long would it take for them to figure out that he'd had the stone with him the entire time? It was a wonder they hadn't known with traitors among them. The secret must have been held by very few. She shook her head to get her racing mind to one side.

"I can't." Her words tumbled out of her mouth. She had never made someone bleed if it wasn't in self-defence or through sheer mistake. Cassidy's hands began to shake.

He held up the knife, like offering a totem to be used in sacrifice. "You can. You said you would take it from here. You're the one who will free this world of its troubles."

"Ohto." Her mouth had dried up incredibly fast. She swallowed with some difficulty. "I can't hurt you."

"You will free me," he begged.

Shouts could be heard, echoing down the passage and into the space of the dead.

Done with asking, he turned the knife around and pressed it to his shirt.

"No." She grabbed at his arms.

"I'll do it for you. Then you can take it for yourself," he assured her.

"No, Ohto. I don't want it," she argued further, straining against his arms, trying to pull them away from the stone in his torso. This was too much.

"Do not lie, Cane. You have always wanted it. From the moment you came here. I saw desire in your face. Determined need. It's all that mattered."

"Not like this," she begged.

Had she caused this? Had she been so driven that she

looked past a boy's need and pushed him to self-sacrifice? There had to be another way.

She struggled against him, locked to a standstill. "Ohto, the people need you," she begged again.

"It doesn't matter what happens to me. This is the best action I can do for them."

"You said you didn't want to give in to your desire to run from power," she snapped back at him.

"Cane," his expression softened, his sunken eyes becoming glassy. They both relaxed in their tug-of-war. "This act will be me wielding all of my power. I will take on the burden to protect this world from the evils that tear into it."

"By dying for them?"

A crash sounded, shaking the room. They lost grip of the blade and it clattered to the floor. Ohto bent to retrieve it. Cassidy caught him by the shoulder, pressing her finger to her lips.

Footsteps echoed louder than the distant sounds of battle. They listened to each patient and purposeful step. Each heel strike fed into Cassidy's sinking sense of unease.

"Nowhere to run, Boy. Bring out the stone and your little Streamer friend," Noh ordered. She sounded more tempered than before. Victory, or confidence in one's victory, could do that.

Cassidy looked into the prince's face, holding his gaze. "I believe," she murmured, pausing to listen for their enemy. They froze in the moment, anticipating words, and fearing attack. The prince waited for the answer, and Cassidy was stuck feeling more than thinking.

It was as though she stood on a precipice. Her heart was thrumming, no longer hammering, but her blood picked up speed none-the-less. "You are worth more alive," she declared before she snatched up the blade and strutted out from behind the statue.

"No. Wait!" he whispered after her. But he was too late.

"Don't worry about him. I've got the stone," she announced loudly.

"No!" Ohto cried. "No, she doesn't," he insisted, racing out from the opposite side.

"Quiet," Cassidy hissed.

Noh laughed despite her battered looking state. Punni had obviously given her a difficult fight. "You speak strangely, Streamer, but your kind has always been...useful," she mused. "Now show me the stone." She held out her hand.

Cassidy took her time, reaching into her jacket with purpose. She stretched out the seconds for as long as she could.

"It's here." Ohto had removed his mail shirt to show the shape protruding from his chest, and the scars that told of how it came to be there.

"Well isn't that novel." She crowed, lighting her hands with magic one final time. She held fog in one and wiry flames in the other.

Cassidy turned her attention to the prince, utterly despondent. If she was responsible for this, having ignored his needs, ignored him through her selfish insistence to race forth and snag even a moment of that rush, then she had to quit her focus to win and show him better now. She had to do whatever she could to reverse the damage she had caused. He needed more time.

Thus, she found herself racing forward, sprinting between them. The magic roared in her ears. She met it in an instant. The force hit her like a freight train. Just as loud, and just as disturbing. The power rocked her clear off her feet.

Hitting the ground didn't stop the thunder inside her chest though. Noh came into her view as the world grew frightfully still. Shock had coloured the witch's pale face. There was something else in her expression as well. Horror?

"Cane," Ohto spoke in a tone that reflected the witch's expression. "What have you done?"

"..." Noh's mouth fell open, but no sound was made. Everything had grown painfully silent.

"Sister Noh," another voice spoke, strong in conviction, but wavering in mortal strength.

Cassidy let her head drop to the side, seeing Pun-ni, one arm limp at his side, legs threatening to fail. His long white hair was now dishevelled and stained with smoke, ash, and blood.

"You have committed the unforgivable sin. You have acted against the laws of our very world." He shook for a moment.

She seemed to know as much. For the first time since Cassidy had met the woman, her angry front had broken. She continued to look down, whether at Cassidy or the floor, she couldn't be sure.

"It is not for us to curb the fate of Streamers." He exhaled, though the breath was unsteady. His remaining mobile arm flickered with magic. The fog was slow to summon forth, and this time it was blacker than night.

"No," Ohto interrupted.

She watched the witch's eyes flicker away from her as a blinding light began to cover them once more. Noh sank to her knees, hands held before her like a prisoner bound. Ohto's magic began to overtake them. However, it failed to impact Cassidy this time. Her body was already preoccupied with its own damage.

"Oh." She realized that fact at last.

CHAPTER EIGHT

"What have you done?"

She woke up warm, with the lingering smell of a freshly lit fire tickling her nose. Cassidy looked at her hands. They were perfectly fine.

"Back again," she heard a voice.

Saka sat down next to her. She was no longer wearing her armour. Her arms were bare, though there were some bandages covering where she had been burned. Her tattered black sash was tied around her waist. Her long hair, half pulled back, tumbled over her shoulders when she leaned forward. "You were incredibly foolish, Cane," she began, her face dour.

Cassidy felt down her torso, finding no pain.

"You could have died. Then we'd be in even more mess." Saka shook her head, more of her hair coming forward.

"What happened?" Cassidy sat up, finding she wasn't even bandaged. Surely she couldn't have dreamed the overwhelming pain.

"He saved you." She crossed her arms and sat back,

like she was satisfied with whatever she saw. "An even enough exchange," she added.

"What?" Cassidy touched the side of her head, not quite keeping up with all she was saying.

"He told me. Everything."

"Oh." She tensed, ready for the hammer to fall.

"How dare you come into our world, into our lives, and seek to destroy our future?" Saka growled.

"Your future? What about his? All this responsibility was killing him," Cassidy argued back, not standing down, even though Saka loomed over her.

"I'm not finished." The formidable guard held up her hand. "You fed into his insecurities. You pulled the loose thread. I can't say why you would do that...I might have called you an enemy, if you hadn't sacrificed yourself like that." She bowed her head. "To your other concern, you should have asked."

"Why?" Cassidy frowned.

"Because I could have told you. I know, without question, that he can do this. He is the only one who can be king," Saka declared.

"What makes you so sure that he can?" Cassidy challenged, ignoring the accusation against her person. She was thinking about the young man this time. Ohto, the brilliant, caring, and sick boy who had been burdened with the weight of the world of the Ohks.

"Because he is my brother."

Saka's statement shocked her into silence. The guard took a moment to bask in the quiet before continuing with her explanation. "Half-brother," she amended. "Same father." She paused again, glancing over Cassidy. "However, I was raised as the household slave. Our father was quite ferocious, you see. But Ohto, he was always kind to me. And he challenged me to learn and grow. He never mistreated me, only ever believed in me. When he was chosen to inherit the seat of Lord Juto the Ascended, he set me free." Saka paused to let all of that sink in. "I sense he might have agreed to be adopted with such eagerness in order to prevail upon the power it gave him. That way he could order my freedom." She smiled.

Cassidy wanted to comment, but it was a lot of heavy information to absorb. She merely blinked, mouth open just a little.

"He encouraged me to work hard, to train, and found me somewhere to go. Two years later, I asked to be his guard. I had gained the skill so no one could challenge me." She concluded, "So, you see, I have no question that he is the best person for the crown. Because he knew how to help me. Most of all, because he wanted to when no one ever taught him how."

"You think a lot of him."

"He is everything." Saka admitted, her eyes focusing into the distance, "Not often is a world graced with such a pure soul. Even less that they are given the chance to make a difference."

She was right. "Okay. I'm sorry."

"He showed you, right?" she looked at Cassidy directly, flicking her long hair back over her shoulder. "He shared the secret of the stone with you?"

Cassidy nodded, keeping as quiet about it as she could.

"We call Lord Juto a god, but Ohto will be more of a

living god than he could ever have hoped to be." She explained, "Ohto and that stone, they're not separate, they
are something else together now." She concluded, wrapping her arms around herself as if needing comfort.

Cassidy stared at her, although she continued to be
preoccupied with the information.

"You were correct in that belief." They both looked to
the open tent flap. Ohto and Pun-ni had arrived.

"We're back." Ohto smirked. He looked taller.

"And?" Saka asked, her gaze on Pun-ni who had a
sling around his arm, but any other damage was covered
by robes.

"Everything checks out. It's more than any scripture
could tell. Certainly, more than I could hope. His solution
to the stone has stabilized it in a fashion my people never
would have dreamed."

"So, you are satisfied?" she inclined her head.

"About that," Ohto piped up, "I have asked Pun-ni to
stay with us. Should I ever become a danger to the people,
he can stabilize the stone...by whatever means necessary."
He spoke with finality.

"Although I don't see why he can't remain alive. Your
words prove true, at least as far as I can see. He is one with
the stone on some level. It's an untold marvel," Pun-ni
told her excitedly.

"While I appreciate that, it doesn't mean I trust you,"
Saka warned him.

"Told you." Ohto smirked.

Pun-ni shrugged his shoulders, ending in a brief
wince.

"He'll also act as an ambassador." Ohto moved his

chin to the side in response to her indignation. It was clear that he was set on this decree and unwilling to negotiate with his sister.

"We'll see," Saka concluded, folding her hands.

"It's time we shared secrets. If we had understood each other properly, this bloodshed might have been mitigated."

Silence passed between the siblings, as they leaned wills against one another.

"We only wanted to stabilize the stone. It's our duty to tame such powers and prevent unthinkable destruction. As I said before, the loss of the Red Kingdom, and the people who had built this temple, the subsequent creation of the dead lands, was all due to the previous Lord Stone that graced our lands." Pun-ni outlined his stance.

Saka dropped her hands and sighed, walking out of the tent.

"She agrees. Just give her time to say it." Ohto smiled then nodded to Pun-ni.

"I'll try not to provoke her." The Ghost Man gave a short bow before taking his leave.

"Cassidy Cane, the promised one." The prince finally addressed her. He still looked pale, and thin. His eyes remained sunken in his head, but she hadn't really noticed that until now because she was wrapped up in the feeling that he had changed.

"How are you holding up?" he seemed older than she remembered too.

"This journey has been incredibly self-informing," she admitted, running her hand through her fiery hair sheepishly.

"I couldn't agree more." He set himself down beside her. "I think it's time I came clean with everything. At least, I'm finding that to be an approach with far greater benefit to me now."

"Alright. By all means," she ushered.

"You see, you came at a time of great change for me. I had just recovered from taking on the stone, which was a short time ago. Only Saka was supposed to know the full truth."

"That it was with you. Literally," Cassidy filled in.

He chuckled, though with a hint of discomfort.

"You remember what I said about the Lord Stone, what it was known to do?"

"It recharged your other magic stones," she said.

"Right."

"But you also said that was among other mysteries," she added.

He smirked. "Ever the clever mind." He mused, "Thank the father for that." His hand drifted to his chest for a brief moment. "The foretelling of your arrival...that was from me."

She cocked her head to the side.

"You witnessed the future come to me." He explained, "When Pun-ni first appeared to us." He touched her jacket that rested beside her bed, feeling the leather for a moment. "They are visions, mostly. Their meanings are incredibly layered and elusive."

"Ah." She nodded, "That's par for the course as I understand it." Out of all the strange and unimaginable things she had encountered in this adventure, soothsaying was one thing she could give a quick reference to.

Most academics studied Cassandra, or they heard of the Oracle of Delphi somewhere along the way.

"I still wish they could be more useful." He rubbed at his neck and shoulder.

"Everything has turned out okay so far," she argued. "And, if you don't mind me saying, I think you'll do very well in the future to come."

"Thank you." He touched her hand before he got up. "Rest. We will be making plans for our next steps soon," he concluded, then left her alone in the tent.

***

News of the battle at the temple seemed to have taken off like wildfire. The prince received word from the capital, which led to a hasty meeting in their large tent.

"It's about time we pulled up stakes and made for the capital," one of Ohto's trusted bannermen began.

"With haste," another chimed in.

Saka sighed before placing a scroll on the table. "Things have changed." She announced, "There's been rebellion in the capital."

"What?" several of the bannermen cried, others gasped.

"General Shoka has written to us with his witness account. He tells of the people rioting, chasing the enemies from the city. Young Toza."

"That plucky captain," someone commented.

"He led his men in and retook the city in the name of our prince," she insisted, smiling.

"And they sent you an invitation?" one man crossed his arms.

"More or less." She nodded.

"How can we trust that this isn't another ambush?" a much younger bannerman worried.

Saka hesitated.

"We don't," Ohto spoke up. "Not entirely. We will advance with caution, send runners and scouts ahead every step of the way. I will ask that we meet again after midday to establish plans should we be betrayed upon returning home."

With that, he had signalled an end to the session. Everyone filed out, leaving him with Saka and Cassidy.

"What can I do?" Cassidy asked, wanting to help them. She should at least try to make up for the mess she'd made for them.

"It's time you returned through your portal," Saka announced.

"What?"

"They don't know it," Ohto glanced to the tent flaps, lowering his voice to protect their secrets, "but the battle is done. We will find no attackers of substance in the capital." He declared, "Of this, I am certain."

"You had a vision?"

"Yes."

"I see." Cassidy felt deflated but she knew the time was right to leave. "I guess I'll start my way back."

Saka snorted, "We're not kicking you out. We're sending you with an escort."

On cue, Vaso entered and bowed to them. "We'll be ready to leave soon."

"We have already decided to establish a permanent settlement at the portal," Ohto said.

CHAPTER NINE

The return trip to the portal went smoothly, making for a dull journey. Cassidy didn't mind though. She got to know more about Vaso, and that he was entrusted with putting down roots near the portal. He was so pleased at the prospect, and that all his relations would meet him there, that his company had been delightful. After travelling on edge the entire time, it was refreshing to hang out with relaxed people who were ready to just live their lives and enjoy a new start.

Vaso took her back to the portal alone and waved her off with a smile.

"I'll be guarding, should you ever return."

"I promise not to come barrelling through next time," she joked, gaining a chuckle from him.

Then he stepped back and watched her march back through the portal and to the woods.

***

After a long hot shower followed by a relaxing bath at the motel, she hopped into her rental car and drove back to the airport. Everything fell into place, and before long she was on a plane back across the country toward home.

After they reached cruising altitude Cassidy set to work, checking her emails. She sent one to Gamgee with the information about her flight. Then she clicked on an email entitled "Research paper assistance." Thinking back, she recalled the young man who had visited her office before she left to see Dr. Gamgee. Trying to recall his features, she could only see those of Prince Ohto. She would do better now. Especially since this student had done as she instructed and emailed her again, looking for a new time to go over his research paper.

She emailed him back, offering a time later today after she settled in, or tomorrow. Then Cassidy switched to her contacts. She scrolled over her family category and looked at Margo's name and photo in the bubble. It was a picture taken from her last work on a production of Grease. Cassidy had snapped the pic of her in a 50's outfit before the stage makeup. Her thumb hovered over the image for a minute or two, before she tapped through and then chose the envelope to take her to the messenger app.

Hey. Maybe you were right. Back in town soon. Dinner?

With all attempts to make amends complete, she put her phone away. She sat back in her seat and waited for time to pass. Feeling particularly restless, however, she soon indulged in a mid-flight movie. Once that was over and she still had a couple hours to go, Cassidy fished a box out of her coat. The craftsmanship was lovely. Its joins were built without nails or screws.

She opened it to study the crest they had given to her. Saka had gifted it to her before they parted. The seal of Ohto's house included a double crown. Between its two layers was the shape of a gem, lines suggesting its magical glow. To Cassidy, the idea was similar to the triple crown of the Papal seal. Below Ohto's heavenly crown were his royal symbols. A sword crossing over a cane in an x-fashion. She touched the x, tracing along the walking stick.

"The one who was promised of Cane," she mused to herself, admiring the mysteries of all worlds.

***

Dr. Herbert Gamgee was at the airport when Cassidy's plane landed. "This is a surprise." She smirked, wondering if he had read her feelings in the tone of her email. Maybe he was here to tell her off. Maybe he would fire her from the project.

"How were the Ohks?" he asked.

"Pretty dangerous." She brushed strands of her hair out of her face.

"I told you." He sipped coffee out of a reusable cup. "Did you get the artifact?"

She stopped as she opened the trunk of her car. How could she explain everything that happened? All her feelings were still running in opposite directions. "It got lost," she admitted.

Silence passed between them.

Still, she waited for the hammer to fall.

But then Gamgee broke out of his statue state and lifted her bag into the trunk for her. "I'm glad you got through alright."

She dared a glance into his face, and found he wasn't angry. At least, not on the surface. If he was angry at all, he was very good at hiding it. "Yeah. Thanks." She stuffed her hands into the pockets of her jacket.

"There's always the next world," he assured her, turning on his heel and walking back to his own car.

"...Yeah." She wasn't sure why she hadn't been completely up front with him about the Lord Stone, but something held her back. All she knew was that it wasn't her ego pulling the strings this time.

She hopped in her car and drove back home. Once she had her things unpacked, she found an email from David, the student from her class. He wanted to meet up in thirty minutes. She was more than willing to help him. He deserved that much. However, by the time she was heading out the door Margo called her back.

"I'm ready for dinner when you are," she insisted, sounding much more amiable.

"Oh," Cassidy bit her lip, hesitating on how to break it to her little sister that she'd have to wait again.

"What is it?" She sounded ready for a let-down.

"You'll have to wait a little. I have a meeting with a student first," she said, scuffing her foot on the doormat gingerly.

"Oh! I don't mind waiting for David." Margo's beaming came through the receiver.

"David?" Cassidy frowned.

"The guy with the research paper," Margo cemented her knowledge. "Take your time, if you have that setting," she joked. "I'll check out your campus library."

"Thanks."

"Anytime, since you're buying."

Cassidy opened her mouth to protest, but the line was already dead. She could only breathe out a chuckle. The point wasn't whether Cassidy had a slower setting or not, it was about the placement of the heart and the head.

EPILOGUE

Tallis awoke with a start, his black hair matted and damp with sweat so much that it clung to the shape of his head.

His black shirt was off and draped over a chair near him. He was in a bed made of long bows of wood with a thin mattress of foam over the top, and the dichotomy of those two things shook him for a moment. He was in a large, gray tent that looked like the type the military sometimes erected.

He looked down at himself.

His chest and stomach were wrapped in gauze and bandages, covering his entire midriff and forming a sash from his left shoulder down around to his right side. He moved to rise, but winced, and made a pained sound.

"I wouldn't move too quick, if I were you," came a haggard voice from outside the door flap.

He stiffened, then loosened as he was joined by an old woman with soft eyes. Her hair was pulled back in a bun so tight that it pulled the skin of her forehead back with it, a permanent facelift. There was a pinch made from tree bark keeping it in place.

Her nostrils were askew, one on each cheek. The slope of her nose continued down into the cleft of her lip, a bump there from when the nostrils had been properly placed somewhere far back on the evolutionary tree.

"You were banged up when we found you. There was an explosion in the forest, and when we went to investigate there were parts all around, and you: not far away. You seemed like you got away from the crash – ejected, maybe – but not far from it." She pointed to his chest. "You punctured your lung."

His hand went gingerly to his solar plexus.

"It's fixed now."

He nodded, remembering the crash. He had been flying a mining pod, escaping the Xik'en asteroid station, when he'd found his way to a portal. He went through to the other side, but had found himself too close to land and unable to veer up in time to miss it, especially with the engines transitioning too quickly from no atmosphere to low. He honestly didn't remember hitting the eject or crawling away, but must have.

His hand went to the side of his face, and felt the gold wiring that lined his jaw where the Branch of Languages still sat. He smiled, then checked his pockets. He seemed panicked for a moment, finding them empty.

"We put it over there," the woman said, motioning to a bedside table.

Tallis turned, seeing his small, thin stress ball on the table. He breathed a sigh of relief and picked it up.

"I'm Clarn," she said, in a tone that indicated he had waited too long to ask.

"Hello, Clarn. I'm Tallis. Thank you for your care."

She smiled and nodded respectfully. She then motioned to the left side of her face, in roughly the same place where the Branch of Languages occupied his. "We tried to remove that but it resisted, and we thought it not best to try again."

"Thank you," he said again, rising from the bed to stand. "I'm on Cortex, then?"

"You shouldn't get up. Your wounds aren't ready," Clarn said, reaching out tentatively.

Tallis checked his wristwatch. The screen was cracked, but it seemed to still be functioning. He pressed the buttons on its side and it bleeped happily. He smiled, sighing in relief. He turned back to Clarn and motioned to her nostrils. "This is Cortex, right?"

She nodded, though she wasn't sure what he meant by the gesture. He was the one that was odd; she wasn't sure how he could tell where she was from by the features everyone had.

"That means the one to the east that leads to Earth is closed..." he mumbled to himself, checking his watch and turning in a slow circle. When he was facing due west it bleeped again. He smiled and pressed another small button along the side. The screen glowed red to indicate it had accepted the command. He grabbed his shirt off of the chair. "I wish I had something to thank you with..."

"It's fine. But you can't go. There's nothing even out there, that way."

He placed a reassuring hand on her shoulder and smiled. "There's at least one thing. Home."

COMING SOON!
THE SNOWS OF AETALUS
BY JD RYOT & SHANNON K GREEN!

The next incredible episode of Slipstreamers, *The Snows of Aetalus*, will be available soon, written with the astonishing Shannon K Green!

Facing uncertainty as her life as a Slipstreamer begins to intrude on her career and a professor and archeologist, Cassidy escapes into a fight against the elements against **The Snows of Aetalus!**

Bestselling author **Shannon K Green** takes Cassidy on this roller coaster novel-length adventure! A not to be missed Slipstreamers extravaganza!

ACKNOWLEDGEMENTS

The authors would like to pay special thanks to the *Slipstreamers* committee at Engen Books, including Amanda Labonté, Matthew LeDrew, Ellen Curtis, Erin Vance, and, Lauralana Dunne.

Without their tireless efforts, none of this would have been possible.

Special thanks to this episode's editor, Ali House.

AJ Ryan would also like to thank her mom for a lifetime of hard work, for always cheering her on, and giving her the push to take on opportunities. Furthermore she gives thanks to her mom for being the first inspiration for every strong female she writes. AJ would also like to extend thanks to Stacey Oakley for her unparalleled advice, support (competition), and friendship.

Lastly, she wishes to thank the Writer's Alliance of Newfoundland and Labrador (WANL) for providing support as well as write-ins, and all her friends in Write Club. Both gave space and time for much of this story to be written.

ON SALE NOW FROM ENGEN BOOKS

"Dunne breathes life into a world of magic and lore that will draw the reader in right up to the epic conclusion. Ashes is a heroic tale not to be missed."
Amanda Labonté
bestselling author of Supenatural Causes

When fifteen-year-old Phoenix loses her caregiver, everyone that she has ever known inexplicably turn their backs on her. Given the impossible burden of repaying an unknown debt, Phoenix sets out on her own with her trusty donkey, Muler, as her only companion. A chance encounter with Malcourt, a mysterious traveller, not only saves her life, but sets it on a trajectory that she would have never thought possible.

ABOUT THE AUTHOR

AJ Ryan is a freelance fiction editor, writer, and artist based in Mount Pearl, Newfoundland. She holds a BA in English from Memorial University of Newfoundland and Labrador and also received a diploma of Independent Illustration from Seneca College.

Ryan is passionate about conveying stories with clarity and creativity. She also works to expand diverse representation in the industry by supporting 2SLGBTQIA+ writers and stories. Along with her freelance editing work, she has been a regular editor with Engen Books since 2018.

JD Ryot is the reclusive creator of the *Slipstreamers* series from Engen Books. JD is an avid fan of young adult literature and adventure serials. When asked if they had come to this world through a portal themselves, JD Ryot refused to answer. No record of their birth has ever been found... on this world.

www.ingramcontent.com/pod-product-compliance
Lightning Source LLC
Chambersburg PA
CBHW032110170626
46808CB00008B/3007